The Really, Really, Really Big Dinosaur

by Richard Byrne

tiger tales

"One for him and one for me.

One for him and one for me."

Jackson was counting out jelly beans
to share with his friend when . . .

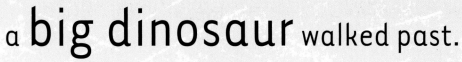
a **big dinosaur** walked past.

"Would you like a jelly bean?"
asked Jackson.

"**I want them all!**"
said the big (and rather rude) dinosaur.

"Oh, I couldn't give them
all to you," said Jackson.
"You see, they belong
to my friend."

"Well, tell your little friend, wherever he is, that I want his jelly beans!"

"He's asleep," said Jackson. "But he's a really, really, really big friend."

"Oh, I'm really, **really, really** scared!" said the big (and rather fresh) dinosaur. "Everyone knows I'm the **biggest** and **strongest** dinosaur around here! Just w-a-i-t and . . .

"You're making
that up,"
said the big dinosaur.
"Anyway, I'm
definitely the best at jumping

"Well, I'd like to see your pretend friend.

or this!"
boasted the big dinosaur.

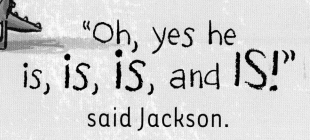

"Oh, yes he
is, is, is, and IS!"
said Jackson.

The big
dinosaur
was getting
angrier
and

angrier . . .

the JELLY BEANS!"

"You can shout as much as you like," said Jackson, "but my friend can shout louder."

"Look here, tinysaur, what **can't** this make-believe friend of yours do?"

Jackson thought for a moment.

"Oh, yes. He's afraid of dark, scary places so he would never go into that cave on his own. . . ."

Just then, the big dinosaur grabbed
the jar of jelly beans and ran into the cave.

"SNAP!"

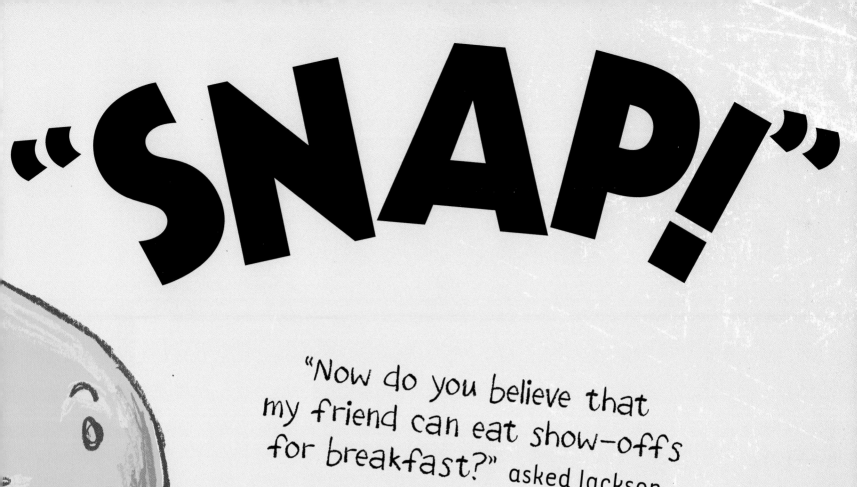

"Now do you believe that my friend can eat show-offs for breakfast?" asked Jackson.

"Yes!" came a small (and really rather sorry) voice from inside.

Jackson giggled. "Don't worry.
He could eat you,
but he won't!"

"JELLY BEANS AND TREETOPS ARE MY FAVORITES!"

said the really, really, really big (and rather friendly) dinosaur

"I won't be a greedy show-off ever again!"

promised the big dinosaur.

"First one to the bottom wins the jelly beans!" called Jackson.

Everyone knew that the big dinosaur was the best at S-l-i-d-i-n-g.

But this time . . .

he was happy just sharing.

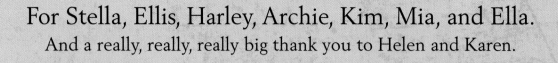

For Stella, Ellis, Harley, Archie, Kim, Mia, and Ella.
And a really, really, really big thank you to Helen and Karen.

tiger tales
an imprint of ME Media, LLC
5 River Road, Suite 128, Wilton, CT 06897
Published in the United States 2012
Originally published in Great Britain in 2012
by Oxford University Press
Text and illustrations copyright © 2012 Richard Byrne
CIP data is available
ISBN-13: 978-1-58925-123-6
ISBN-10: 1-58925-123-7
Printed in China
LPP0112
1 3 5 7 9 10 8 6 4 2

For more insight and activities,
visit us at www.tigertalesbooks.com